11/15/12

Julie Andrews'
Treasury
For All
Seasons

Poems *and* Songs *to* Celebrate *the* Year

Selected by Julie Andrews & Emma Walton Hamilton

Paintings by Marjorie Priceman

L B

LITTLE, BROWN AND COMPANY
NEW YORK   BOSTON

Contents

SPRING ....

MARCH

APRIL

MAY

FALL ....

SEPTEMBER

OCTOBER

NOVEMBER

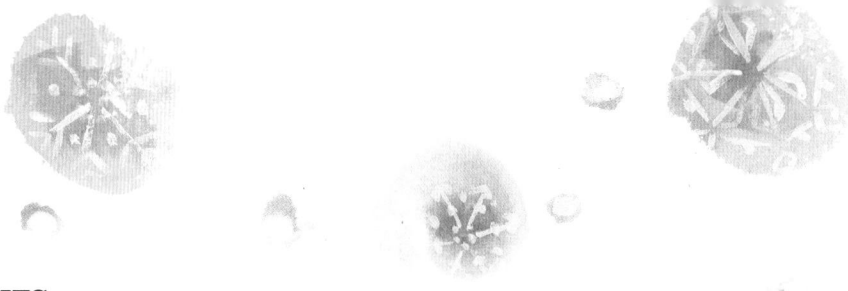

DECEMBER LIGHTS ....

DECEMBER

OTHER CELEBRATIONS & SPECIAL OCCASIONS ....

THE SABBATH/SHABBAT

BIRTHDAYS

NEW BABIES

COMING OF AGE/RITES OF PASSAGE

HOLIDAYS & CELEBRATIONS & THEIR CORRESPONDING POEMS

The Day Is Done

Come, read to me some poem,
    Some simple and heartfelt lay,
That shall soothe this restless feeling,
    And banish the thoughts of day.

Not from the grand old masters,
    Not from the bards sublime,
Whose distant footsteps echo
    Through the corridors of Time.

For, like strains of martial music,
    Their mighty thoughts suggest
Life's endless toil and endeavor;
    And tonight I long for rest.

Read from some humbler poet,
    Whose songs gushed from his heart,
As showers from the clouds of summer,
    Or tears from the eyelids start;

Who, through long days of labor,
And nights devoid of ease,
Still heard in his soul the music
Of wonderful melodies.

Such songs have power to quiet
The restless pulse of care,
And come like the benediction
That follows after prayer.

Then read from the treasured volume
The poem of thy choice,
And lend to the rhyme of the poet
The beauty of thy voice.

And the night shall be filled with music
And the cares, that infest the day,
Shall fold their tents, like the Arabs,
And as silently steal away.

Henry Wadsworth Longfellow
(Abridged version)

11

When my daughter Emma and I began compiling this book, we studied several different calendars to obtain a better understanding of all the holidays we celebrate on our small, diverse planet. It was rather a surprise to discover there were so many more than we had imagined. One year is *packed* with possibilities for celebration!

Our first anthology, *Julie Andrews' Collection of Poems, Songs, and Lullabies*, was all about our family favorites—poems and songs we'd shared and loved over many generations. While there are plenty of further favorites in this collection, many of them are *new* ones...and what a pleasure it has been to research and discover them!

Great lyrics are poems, and nothing could please me more than if you, dear reader, upon reading the words, would feel moved to discover the accompanying melody.

We found as we worked that a number of gifted poets resurfaced again and again. It ceased to be a surprise when, having found a poem we adored, we discovered it was by Myra Cohn Livingston, Rachel Field, Jack Prelutsky, Barbara Juster Esbensen, John Mole, David McCord, Lilian Moore, or Marchette Chute.

The same is true of lyricists. It was always a delight when, researching a particular topic, we found that one of our favorite songwriters had penned the perfect sentiment for just such a moment. Great lyrics *are* poems, and nothing could please me more than if you, dear reader, upon reading the words, would feel moved to discover the accompanying melody.

At the end of this book, you will find Rudyard Kipling's great poem "If." Kipling says:

> "If you can fill the unforgiving minute
> With sixty seconds' worth of distance run,
> Yours is the Earth and everything that's in it."

It seems to me that this is the essence of what great poets and lyricists do. They capture a moment—reveal a new perspective for us and, in so doing, advance our knowledge of the world and of ourselves.

Now, *that's* something to celebrate!

A Year

The Months

January brings the snow,
Makes our feet and fingers glow.

February brings the rain,
Thaws the frozen lake again.

March brings breezes loud and shrill,
Stirs the dancing daffodil.

April brings the primrose sweet,
Scatters daisies at our feet.

May brings flocks of pretty lambs,
Skipping by their fleecy dams.

June brings tulips, lilies, roses,
Fills the children's hands with posies.

Hot July brings cooling showers,
Apricots and gillyflowers.

August brings the sheaves of corn,
Then the harvest home is borne.

Warm September brings the fruit,
Sportsmen then begin to shoot.

Fresh October brings the pheasant,
Then to gather nuts is pleasant.

Dull November brings the blast,
Then the leaves are whirling fast.

Chill December brings the sleet,
Blazing fire, and Christmas treat.

Sara Coleridge

Winter

*I*n our family, we love to celebrate the promise of a new year with a long walk. No matter the weather or location—be it the mountains, beach, woods, or city—the world seems filled with potential on New Year's Day.

"The snow on the trees waits for company."

Of course, winter is far from over, and as a dear mountain-man friend of ours says, "The snow on the trees waits for company." It's a prediction of more snow to come and an invitation to go out and play. Opportunities abound for skating on the local ponds, sledding at the school hill, building snowmen, and engaging in any number of other wonderful winter activities.

The snow is such a lovely canvas for nature. Every twig seems outlined, every bird a pristine work of art against the white. Cardinals are frequent visitors to our gardens, which is why Barbara Juster Esbensen's lovely poem "Cardinal" resonates for us both. "Red as a shout," the one in my garden seems to fancy its own image. It admires itself in the side-view mirror of my car, and taps on our window when it's time to be fed. The one at Emma's house nests in the yew tree near her living-room window and is inclined to peck at its own reflection, thinking it's another cardinal intruding upon its territory. We feed the birds

year-round, but in the wintertime the activity brings our family added pleasure. Time permitting, we could sit for hours and watch the passing parade.

Our cats and dogs seem to appreciate the snow as much as Myra Cohn Livingston's do in "Kittens." Emma's Golden Doodle, Louie, loves nothing more than to root in the snowdrifts and surface, blinking and bewhiskered, his caramel-colored beard turned white. My beloved miniature poodles disappear almost entirely, then re-emerge, leaping like gazelles as they traverse the garden in frisky delight.

We've never made valentines for our dogs as Jack Prelutsky tried to do, but Valentine's Day *is* prime poem season in our household. One of my other daughters, Amelia, celebrates her birthday on Valentine's Day, so it's a great occasion for flowers, cards, collages, gifts, expressions of affection in poetic form, and, of course, extra chocolates (of which she is *very* fond).

When you consider New Year's Day, Martin Luther King Day, Groundhog Day, Chinese New Year, Valentine's Day, Mardi Gras, and Presidents' Day, the months of January and February are packed tight with celebrations—plenty of opportunities for "a wet and merry end of day," such as the one in Karen Gundersheimer's evocative poem "Happy Winter, Steamy Tub"!

New Year's Day

Last night, while we were fast asleep,
The old year went away.
It can't come back again because
A new one's come to stay.

Rachel Field

New Year's Resolutions

Last year I did some rotten things.
This year I will be better.
Here are some resolutions
I will follow to the letter:

I won't make dumb excuses
when my homework isn't done;
when the truth is that I did no work
'cause I was having fun.

I won't fly paper airplanes
when the teacher isn't looking.
I won't sneak in the kitchen
just to taste what they are cooking.

I will not twist the silverware
to see how far it bends.
I will not take the candy bars
from lunch bags of my friends.

I will not skateboard down the hall
or skateboard down the stairs.
I won't run over teachers,
and I won't crash into chairs.

I will not do these rotten things;
my heart is full of sorrow.
But I have got some brand-new tricks
to try in school tomorrow.

Bruce Lansky

Martin Luther King Day

The dream
of Martin Luther King
will happen
in some far-off Spring

when winter ice
and snow are gone.
One day, the dreamer
in gray dawn

will waken
to a blinding light
where hawk and dove
in silent flight

brush wings together
on a street
still thundering
with ghostly feet.

And soul will dance
and soul will sing
and march with
Martin Luther King.

Myra Cohn Livingston

I Dream a World

I dream a world where man
No other man will scorn,
Where love will bless the earth
And peace its paths adorn.
I dream a world where all
Will know sweet freedom's way,
Where greed no longer saps the soul
Nor avarice blights our day.
A world I dream where black or white,
Whatever race you be,
Will share the bounties of the earth
And every man is free,
Where wretchedness will hang its head
And joy, like a pearl,
Attends the needs of all mankind—
Of such I dream, my world!

Langston Hughes

The Last Word of a Bluebird
As Told to a Child

As I went out a Crow
In a low voice said, "Oh,
I was looking for you.
How do you do?
I just came to tell you
To tell Lesley (will you?)
That her little Bluebird
Wanted me to bring word
That the north wind last night
That made the stars bright
And made ice on the trough
Almost made him cough
His tail feathers off.
He just had to fly!
But he sent her Good-by,
And said to be good,
And wear her red hood,
And look for the skunk tracks
In the snow with an ax—
And do everything!
And perhaps in the spring
He would come back and sing."

Robert Frost

24

Cardinal

Red as a shout
he stamps himself
like a Chinese signature
on the clean snow
under the dark juniper tree
in the park.

He is a scarlet stroke
of ink
brushed in—
a feathered ending
to a poem about
snow.

In the whole city
pale and dusted with
snow
only his wings are ablaze
with poppies!

Barbara Juster Esbensen

The Snowflake

Before I melt,
Come look at me!
This lovely icy filigree!
Of a great forest
In one night
I make a wilderness
Of white:
By skyey cold
Of crystals made,
All softly, on
Your finger laid,
I pause, that you
My beauty see:
Breathe, and I vanish
Instantly.

Walter de la Mare

White Fields

1.
In the winter time we go
Walking in the fields of snow;

Where there is no grass at all;
Where the top of every wall,

Every fence and every tree,
Is as white as white can be.

2.
Pointing out the way we came,
Everyone of them the same—

All across the fields there be
Prints in silver filigree;

And our mothers always know,
By our footprints in the snow,

Where the children go.

James Stephens

Kittens

Our cat had kittens
weeks ago
when everything outside was snow.

So she stayed in
and kept them warm
and safe from all the clouds and storm.

But yesterday
when there was sun
she snuzzled on the smallest one

and turned it over
from beneath
and took its fur between her teeth

and carried it
outside to see
how nice a winter day can be

and then our dog
decided he
would help her take the other three

and one by one
they took them out
to see what sun is all about

so when they're grown
they'll always know
to never be afraid of snow.

Myra Cohn Livingston

Skating

When I try to skate,
My feet are so wary
They grit and they grate:
And then I watch Mary
Easily gliding,
Like an ice-fairy;
Skimming and curving,
Out and in,
With a turn of her head,
And a lift of her chin,
And a gleam of her eye,
And a twirl and a spin;
Sailing under
The breathless hush
Of the willows, and back
To the frozen rush;
Out to the island
And round the edge,
Skirting the rim
Of the crackling sedge,
Swerving close
To the poplar root,
And round the lake
On a single foot,
With a three, and an eight,
And a loop and a ring;
Where Mary glides,
The lake will sing!
Out in the mist
I hear her now
Under the frost
Of the willow-bough
Easily sailing,
Light and fleet,
With the song of the lake
Beneath her feet.

Herbert Asquith

Happy Winter, Steamy Tub

Happy Winter, steamy tub
To soak and splash in, wash and rub.
Big blobs of bubbles pile on me
The way the snow sits on a tree.
I rinse the soap off, scrub some more,
Drip puddles on the bathroom floor—
Then gurgling bubbles drain away,
A wet and merry end of day.

Karen Gundersheimer

February

Ground Hog Day

Ground Hog sleeps
All winter
Snug in his fur,
Dreams
Green dreams of
Grassy shoots,
Of nicely newly nibbly
Roots—
Ah, he starts to
Stir.
With drowsy
Stare
Looks from his burrow
Out on fields of
Snow.
What's there?
Oh no.
His shadow. Oh,
How sad!
Six more
Wintry
Weeks
To go.

Lilian Moore

New Year's Day!

New Year's Day!
Noodles for breakfast,
sweet rice cakes.
A red envelope stuffed with money
in my pocket.
And lions in the street outside.
I fly downstairs to be there
when they come—
leaping, pouncing,
prancing, roaring,
jumping, dancing,
shaking their neon manes.
Drums beat
feet stamp
hands clap
voices shout
Chinatown,
this is Chinatown!

Kam Mak

Chinese New Year
Traditional Chinese Nursery Rhyme

You'll find whenever the New Year comes
The Kitchen God will want some plums.
The girls will want some flowers new;
The boys will want firecrackers, too.
A new felt cap will please papa,
And a sugar cake for dear mama.

Anonymous

To You

I think I could walk
through the simmering sand
if I held your hand.
I think I could swim
the skin shivering sea
if you would accompany me.
And run on ragged, windy heights,
climb rugged rocks
and walk on air.

I think I could do anything at all,
if you were there.

Karla Kuskin

I Made My Dog a Valentine

I made my dog a valentine,
she sniffed it very hard,
then chewed on it a little while
and left it in the yard.

I made one for my parrakeets,
a pretty paper heart,
they pulled it with their claws
    and beaks
until it ripped apart.

I made one for my turtle,
all *he* did was get it wet,
I wonder if a valentine
is wasted on a pet.

Jack Prelutsky

A Valentine

A Valentine must have a heart
To convey the loving part
Of one, I'm told.
Well, if I could but have my way
Upon this somewhat special day
I'd be original. And bold.

A heart seems far too small a thing
To carry all the love I bring
To you. No, truly.
So, I'd curl myself upon this page
Despite my hefty size and age
And sign it.
Your unruly
But <u>very</u> loving
Julie.

Julie Andrews

Ode to Us

How fine
The years with you (now nine)
Will be, and are...like wine
Improving yearly
By design.

Like puzzle pieces
We combine
So perfectly that to define
The ways in which our hearts entwine
Would be to capture
The Divine
(Or maybe it's our souls?
A sign
That all our planets do align...)

Allow me, then, to thus opine:
Our love will ever grow
And shine
Upon the world.
The bottom line
Is if you'll stay forever mine
Then I,
Eternally,
Am thine.

Emma Walton Hamilton

In Fancy Dress
(It'll be a la-di-dah Mardi Gras)

We're invited to a party
Me and Milly
(Mill's me girl)
A fancy dress-up Mardi Gras affair
We've thought about it often
And we're really in a whirl
For we still can't quite agree on
What to wear

Mill wants to wear her feather boas
So she thinks that I should go as
Some romantic antic hero
Such as Harlequin or Pierrot
And Milly'd be some silly frilly doll
But I won't be a prancing prankster
I've decided—many thanks—to
Be a gangster
Coddling Milly
As me Moll

        (Well—my Milly likes to be molly-coddled)

I'll wear black and in my fist'll
Be a dagger or a pistol
I'll turn up my raincoat collar
Borrow someone's silver dollar
Then I'll loll about and spin it through the air

Or I'll ask my father
When he's in a good mood—for a penny—
If he's any—
If he hasn't
I don't care

(I'll just spin a button or something)

Milly—doll'd up in mascara
Feathers and a glass tiara
Will be far away
The best-dressed at the ball
She'll just stand there
Then I'll dash in
With me eyes and teeth all flashin'
And I'll smother Mill with passion
As the drums and things are crashin'
Loud as loud—and cymbals clashin'
We'll be smashin'...
We'll be smashin'...

(What's that Mill?...No passion?)

Oh!...Perhaps I'll go as Pierrot after all!

Tony Walton

George Washington's Birthday: Wondering

I wonder what I would have said
if my dad asked me,
"Son, do you know who cut down
my pretty cherry tree?"
I think I might have closed my eyes
and thought a little bit
about the herds of elephants
I'd seen attacking it.
I would have heard the rat-a-tat
of woodpeckers, at least,
or the raging roar of a charging boar
or some such other beast!
Perhaps a hippopotamus
with nothing else to do
had wandered through our garden
and stopped to take a chew.
We all know George said,
"Father, I cannot tell a lie."
Yet I can't help but wonder...
Did he *really* try?

Bobbi Katz

Abraham Lincoln

Remember he was poor and country-bred;
His face was lined; he walked with awkward gait.
Smart people laughed at him sometimes and said,
"How can so very plain a man be great?"

Remember he was humble, used to toil.
Strong arms he had to build a shack, a fence,
Long legs to tramp the woods, to plow the soil,
A head chuck full of backwoods common sense....

Remember that his eyes could light with fun;
That wisdom, courage, set his name apart;
But when the rest is duly said and done,
Remember that men loved him for his heart.

Mildred Meigs

We Cannot All Be
Washingtons and Lincolns

We cannot all be Washingtons and Lincolns
And have our birthdays celebrated
But we can love the things they loved,
And we can hate the things they hated.

They loved the truth, they hated lies.
They minded what their mothers taught them
And every day they tried to do
The simple duties that it brought them.

Perhaps the reason little folks
Are sometimes great when they grow taller
Is because, like General George and Honest Abe,
They did their best when they were smaller!

Anonymous

Spring

*F*rom the thunderstorms of March through April showers to the miracle of May, there is so much to "praise" about spring, as Eleanor Farjeon tells us in her lovely "Morning has broken."

We're both great fans of the lyricist Johnny Mercer, and his "A Little Boy's Rainy Day" perfectly captures our own pleasure in the coziness of rain. What's better than having "a great big book, an apple, 'n' games to play" and curling up by the fire? When Emma was little and scared of thunder, I used to tell her—as my mother told me—that God was just moving his furniture around. It always helped, and Emma now uses the same tactic with her own kids (though she's inclined to say God's bowling instead!).

Though we haven't a shred of Irish in our heritage, we've always had an affinity for Ireland and for Irish people (and, as Jenny Whitehead aptly says of St. Patrick's Day, "Not Irish? No matter . . . Ye're Irish today!"). We have *many* Irish friends, some so close as to be considered family, and it's absolutely true that "when Irish eyes are smiling . . . they steal your heart away." We once lived in Ireland for four months while my husband and I were making a film. That happy spring and summer provided such inspiration that I wrote my first children's book, *Mandy*, based on our experiences there.

The celebrations of Passover and Easter bring crocuses and daffodils, hunts for eggs and afikomen, special

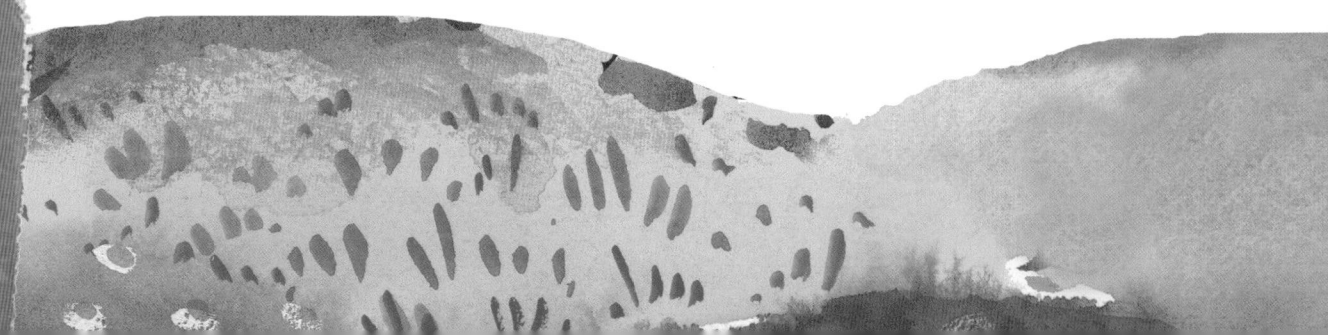

holiday foods and traditions ... and *more* poems. My children and I once enjoyed an early spring lunch on our balcony, just days before Easter. The sun was warm, though snow was still on the ground, and suddenly we saw a large hare bounding along the field below us. It was in such a hurry that we agreed it *must* have been the Easter Bunny.

The celebrations of Passover and Easter bring crocuses and daffodils, hunts for eggs and afikomen, special holiday foods and traditions ... and more *poems.*

A day that gives me special pleasure is Arbor Day. "What Do We Plant?" reminds me of my father, who was a "tree hugger" to his core, as am I. I'm happy to say that my grandson Sam has inherited that gene, for he loves to wrap his arms around a tree as much as climb one.

With five children, I could probably fill a whole book on Mother's Day alone! One particularly happy memory is when three of my daughters offered me a "spa day." It turned out to be a "home" spa: a shoulder rub from Joanna, a pedicure from Amelia, breakfast served by Jenny, all at the same time. I smiled for the rest of the day, in spite of having to deal with the cleanup later!

March

The sun is nervous
As a kite
That can't quite keep
Its own string tight.

Some days are fair,
And some are raw.
The timid earth
Decides to thaw.

Shy budlets peep
From twigs on trees,
And robins join
The chickadees.

Pale crocuses
Poke through the ground
Like noses come
To sniff around.

The mud smells happy
On our shoes.
We still wear mittens,
Which we lose.

John Updike

Morning has broken

Morning has broken
Like the first morning,
Blackbird has spoken
   Like the first bird.
      Praise for the singing!
      Praise for the morning!
      Praise for them, springing
         Fresh from the Word!

Sweet the rain's new fall
Sunlit from heaven,
Like the first dewfall
   On the first grass.
      Praise for the sweetness
      Of the wet garden,
      Sprung in completeness
         Where his feet pass.

Mine is the sunlight!
Mine is the morning
Born of the one light
   Eden saw play!
      Praise with elation,
      Praise every morning,
      God's re-creation
         Of the new day!

Eleanor Farjeon

When Irish Eyes Are Smiling

When Irish eyes are smiling,
Sure, it's like a morn in Spring.
In the lilt of Irish laughter,
You can hear the angels sing.
When Irish hearts are happy,
All the world seems bright and gay.
And when Irish eyes are smiling,
Sure, they steal your heart away.

For your smile is a part,
Of the love in your heart...
And it makes even sunshine more bright.
Like the linnets' sweet song,
Crooning all the day long,
Comes your laughter so tender and light.
For the springtime of life
Is the sweetest of all,
There is ne'er a real care or regret;
And while springtime is ours
Throughout all of youth's hours,
Let us smile each chance we get.

Lyrics by Chauncey Olcott and Geo. Graff Jr.
Music by Ernest R. Ball
(Abridged version)

On St. Patrick's Day

A "Top of the Morning!"
Child, where is your green?
From my head to my feet,
I am green in between!
Got my leprechaun hat
And my shamrock balloon,
'Tis an Irish parade
Passing by here at noon.
Aye, soda bread's baking
Corned beef's in the pot,
I'm dancing a jig—
My feet, they won't stop!
A toast to good health—
Lift your green milk—*SLAINTE!*
Not Irish? No matter...
Ye're Irish today!

Jenny Whitehead

The Fourteenth Day of Adar

See the spring sky
full of kites and small birds!

Our kitchen
fragrant
with honey and poppyseed
fills up with fat little
three-cornered pies—*Hamantaschen!*

Tonight
in my long dress I will be
Esther the Queen.
Tonight
on a small stage I will save
my people. I will remember
my lines.

"There he crawls!" I will say
to the King.
"There he crawls—in his
three-cornered hat—the serpent, Haman!"

Come into our Purim kitchen
and nibble the three-cornered
hats—sweet to recall
a sweet queen, a sweet victory,
a wicked man   gone!

Barbara Juster Esbensen

54

Spring

I'm shouting
I'm singing
I'm swinging through trees
I'm winging skyhigh
With the buzzing black bees.
I'm the sun
I'm the moon
I'm the dew on the rose.
I'm a rabbit
Whose habit
Is twitching his nose.
I'm lively
I'm lovely
I'm kicking my heels.
I'm crying "Come dance"
To the fresh water eels.
I'm racing through meadows
Without any coat
I'm a gamboling lamb
I'm a light leaping goat
I'm a bud
I'm a bloom
I'm a dove on the wing.
I'm running on rooftops
And welcoming spring!

Karla Kuskin

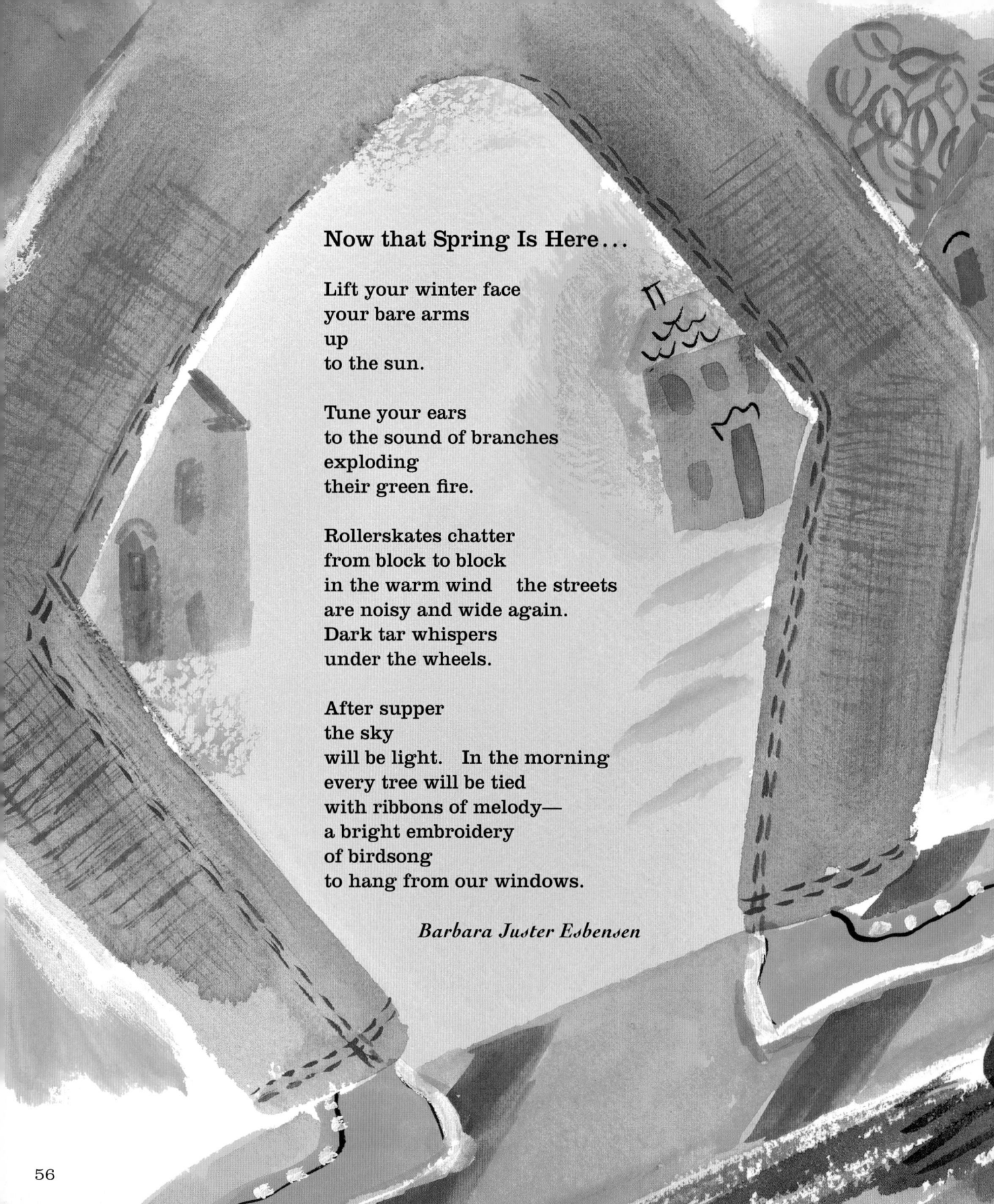

Now that Spring Is Here...

Lift your winter face
your bare arms
up
to the sun.

Tune your ears
to the sound of branches
exploding
their green fire.

Rollerskates chatter
from block to block
in the warm wind   the streets
are noisy and wide again.
Dark tar whispers
under the wheels.

After supper
the sky
will be light.   In the morning
every tree will be tied
with ribbons of melody—
a bright embroidery
of birdsong
to hang from our windows.

Barbara Juster Esbensen

April Fool

The maple syrup's full of ants.
    A mouse is creeping on the shelf.

      Is that a spider on your back?
I ate the whole pie by myself.

The kitchen sink just overflowed.
    A flash flood washed away the school.
I threw your blanket in the trash.

     I never lie———I———
        APRIL FOOL!

        Myra Cohn Livingston

April

April

The roofs are shining from the rain,
    The sparrows twitter as they fly,
And with a windy April grace
    The little clouds go by.

Yet the back-yards are bare and brown
    With only one unchanging tree—
I could not be so sure of Spring
    Save that it sings in me.

Sara Teasdale

A Little Boy's Rainy Day

I'm gettin' tired o' all o' this sunshine—
How I'd love to spend a little boy's rainy day!
Coat around my shoulder,
Wind a-blowin' colder,
Swirlin' all the leaves in a kind of whirly way;
Ol' tin-roof attic drummin' above me—
Got a great big book,
An apple, 'n' games to play.
When it starts to thunder,
Let the grown-ups wonder
What I'm up to under
A bed or in the hay.
Hey, I'm eatin' stuff 'n' gettin' fatter,
'N' feelin' warm as pancake batter,
'N' watchin' puddle jumpers scatterin' on their way.
Seein' all the raindrops patterin',
Hearin' thunder rat-tat-tatterin',
Scared to bits but that don't matter, 'n'
I'm okay.
Let the raindrops pitter-patter,
Let the lightnin' play,
Let the thunder boom and roll away!
Say, I'm havin' me a windowpaney,
Hurricaney, weathervaney,
Take-a-look-I-betcha-couldn't-find-me
Little boy's rainy day!

Lyrics by Johnny Mercer
Music by David Saxon

Umbrellas

Umbrellas bloom
Along our street
Like flowers on a stem.
And almost everyone
I meet
Is holding one of them.

Under my umbrella-top,
Splashing through the town,
I wonder why the tulips
Hold umbrellas
Up-side-down!

Barbara Juster Esbensen

Passover

Out of a land
that held us slaves,

Under the wings
of the angel of death,

Over hot sands,
across cold seas,

We sing again
with freedom's breath.

Myra Cohn Livingston

63

Chief Seattle's Lesson

Seattle was a teacher
Who taught us how to care
For all the living things on earth,
Fresh water, and clean air.
"The earth does not belong to us,"
Great Chief Seattle said.
"We sometimes think it does, but we
Belong to earth, instead."

Helen H. Moore

What Do We Plant?

What do we plant when we plant the tree?
We plant the ship, which will cross the sea.
We plant the mast to carry the sails;
We plant the planks to withstand the gales—
The keel, the keelson, the beam, the knee;
We plant the ship when we plant the tree.

What do we plant when we plant the tree?
We plant the houses for you and me.
We plant the rafters, the shingles, the floors,
We plant the studding, the lath, the doors,
The beams and siding, all parts that be;
We plant the house when we plant the tree.

What do we plant when we plant the tree?
A thousand things that we daily see;
We plant the spire that out-towers the crag,
We plant the staff for our country's flag,
We plant the shade, from the hot sun free;
We plant all these when we plant the tree.

Henry Abbey

Our Tree

When spring comes round, our apple tree
    Is very full of flowers,
And when a bird sits on a branch
    The petals fall in showers.

When summer comes, our apple tree
    Is very full of green,
And everywhere you look in it
    There is a leafy screen.

When autumn comes, our apple tree
    Is full of things to eat.
The apples hang from every branch
    To tumble at our feet.

When winter comes, our apple tree
    Is full of snow and ice
And rabbits come to visit it...
    We think our tree is nice.

Marchette Chute

A Tree Outside My Window

I have some work to do,
But I don't feel like doing work today.
The sky is far too blue,
And spring is calling me to come and play.
My conscience tells me I must ignore it
And if I'm strong and firm
I'll feel the better for it.
And then a breeze comes up
And blows my good intentions all away.

A tree outside my window
Is waving its leaves at me
As if to say,
"It's a lovely day,
Come out, come out and see."
A bird outside my window
Is singing upon the tree.
His songs all say:
"It's a lovely day,
Come out, come out and see.
You can pass up work and worry
For more important things,
You can throw a stone in the middle of a brook
And watch the water make rings!
There's sunlight on the meadow,
You can see it right through the tree.
The world is gay,
It's a lovely day,
Come out, come out and see for yourself,
Come out, come out and see!"

*Lyrics and music by Oscar Hammerstein II
and William Hammerstein II*

May

Now children may
    Go out of doors,
Without their coats,
    To candy stores.

The apple branches
    And the pear
May float their blossoms
    Through the air,

And Daddy may
    Get out his hoe
To plant tomatoes
    In a row,

And, afterwards,
    May lazily
Look at some baseball
    On TV.

John Updike

Bee, I'm expecting you!

Bee, I'm expecting you!
Was saying yesterday
To somebody you know
That you were due.

The frogs got home last week,
Are settled and at work,
Birds mostly back,
The clover warm and thick.

You'll get my letter by
The seventeenth; reply,
Or better, be with me.
    Yours,
      Fly.

Emily Dickinson

The First Dandelion

Simple and fresh and fair from winter's close emerging,
As if no artifice of fashion, business, politics, had ever been,
Forth from its sunny nook of shelter'd grass—innocent,
    golden, calm as the dawn,
The spring's first dandelion shows its trustful face.

Walt Whitman

Dancing Paper

Let's fill the room with laughing
before our friends arrive.
We'll bring the colored paper.
The room will come alive.

Let's start with the *piñata*.[1]
The air will sway and swing.
We'll string *papel picado*[2]
to start its fluttering.

I'll fling the *serpentinas*,[3]
toss coils in the air.
We'll add *marimba*[4] music,
start dancing everywhere.

Remember *cascarones*,[5]
to hide will be in vain.
Egg-bursts of bright confetti
will shower us like rain.

Pat Mora

[1] A brightly colored paper container filled with candy or toys that is used to celebrate special occasions

[2] "Punched paper"—a popular Mexican art form in which designs are cut into paper and used to make flags and banners

[3] Mexican paper accordions used as banners or streamers

[4] A wooden musical instrument that is similar to a xylophone

[5] Confetti eggs; festive, hollow eggshells filled with confetti

**Breakfast in Bed For
Mother's Day!**

We cooked Mom scrambled eggs
(and dropped some on the floor).

We made her buttered toast
(and smeared the kitchen door).

We flipped a dozen pancakes
(now two are on the ceiling).

We sliced up a banana
(I think we lost the peeling).

We poured the maple syrup
(it's dripping down the chairs).

Happy Mother's Day, Mom.
(Well, *if* you stay upstairs!)

Jenny Whitehead

Mama, A Rainbow

What do you give to the lady who has given
    all her life and love to you?
What do you give to the reasons you are
    livin'?
I could windowshop the world
    before I'm through

Mama, a rainbow,
Mama, a sunrise,
Mama, the moon to wear.
That's not good enough,
no, not good enough.
Not for Mama.

Mama, a palace.
Diamonds like doorknobs.
Mountains of gold to spare.
That's not rich enough,
no, not rich enough,
not for Mama.

Mama, a lifetime, crowded with laughter,
that's not long enough,
not half long, enough

What can I give you
that I can give you?
What will your present be?
Mama young and beautiful,
always young and beautiful.
That's the Mama I'll always see.
That's for Mama
with love from me.

Lyrics by Hal Hackady
Music by Larry Grossman

75

Memorial Day

Daddy keeps the war in a shoebox
  tied up tight
       with a long white string.

On Memorial Day
  we open the box
      lift the lid
        and look inside.

Dog tags and pins and stars and stripes
all jumbled together like prizes in a gumball machine.

    Then Daddy puts my hands in his
    and tells me about the war

And I feel the meaning of Memorial Day

     in the warmth of Daddy's hands.

Constance Andrea Keremes

Summer

*I*t often seems that, overnight, spring has gone and summer is upon us, with all the wonders of that golden season. The days seem to stretch out ahead, filled with invitations to enjoy the great outdoors.

I love the references in Katrina Porteous' "Skylark" to "pure joy in a shower of bubbles" and "the warmth of the sun in a song." These days, skylarks are rather rare—but as a child in England, I always marveled when I saw one hovering above a field in full-throated song. How something so small and plain could sustain such a beautiful sound while in motion was a source of inspiration to me.

Father's Day is, of course, another opportunity for celebration. Folami Abiade's image of being closer to the sun when "in daddy's arms" is so lovely and poignant. Emma and her children created a book called *We Love Daddy Because...* and add new thoughts and insights to it every Father's Day. It's adorable to see the progression of the children's love for their dad over the years, from the early "He plays roughhouse" and "Candyland" and "He mows the lawn with me" entries, to the more recent "He plays baseball" and "music" and "He builds Ancient Roman lawn mowers (a school project!) with me."

Whether it's early childhood, elementary school, middle school, high school, or college, graduation is a tremulous but triumphant time. If one is asked to be a speaker, there is a huge responsibility to get it right. I hope that some of our selections for this section may help put things in perspective or perhaps provide a little inspiration. We particularly admire Joy Harjo's list of things to "Remember," especially "the dance language is, that life is."

We had such fun finding poems about all our favorite summer activities—swimming, riding bikes, climbing trees, fishing, eating and sleeping outside, spotting fireflies. Myra Cohn Livingston's "Reading: Summer" says it all. Carefree, careless days with the pleasure of having no schedule...

We had such fun finding poems about all our favorite summer activities — swimming, riding bikes, climbing trees, fishing, eating and sleeping outside, spotting fireflies.

And, of course, there's baseball. I am British, and it took me a while to warm up to the sport—but one passionate grandson changed it all for me. Everyone in our family is now a die-hard baseball fan! Sam devotes his entire summer to this great American pastime, coaching at a baseball camp, pitching for his school team, and, of course, going to games whenever time and resources permit. May Swenson's "Analysis of Baseball" brilliantly sums up what the sport's all about—although for us, it's also about discipline, teamwork, courage, excellence...and heroes.

June

The sun is rich
    And gladly pays
In golden hours,
    Silver days,

And long green weeks
    That never end.
School's out. The time
    Is ours to spend.

There's Little League,
    Hopscotch, the creek,
And, after supper,
    Hide-and-seek.

That live-long light
    Is like a dream,
And freckles come
    Like flies to cream.

John Updike

Skylark

Suddenly above the fields you're pouring
Pure joy in a shower of bubbles,
Lacing the spring with the blue thread of summer.
You're the warmth of the sun in a song.

You're light spun to a fine filament;
Sun on a spider-thread—
That delicate.

You're the lift and balance the soul feels,
The terrible, tremulous, uncertain thrill of it—
You're all the music the heart needs,
Full of its sudden fall, silent fields

Katrina Porteous

Today

If ever there were a spring day so perfect,
so uplifted by a warm intermittent breeze

that it made you want to throw
open all the windows in the house

and unlatch the door to the canary's cage,
indeed, rip the little door from its jamb,

a day when the cool brick paths
and the garden bursting with peonies

seemed so etched in sunlight
that you felt like taking

a hammer to the glass paperweight
on the living room end table,

releasing the inhabitants
from their snow-covered cottage

so they could walk out,
holding hands and squinting

into this larger dome of blue and white,
well, today is just that kind of day.

Billy Collins

Flags

Why do we salute a flag,
A vibrant, colorful piece of rag?
Certainly it suggests, to me,
A piece of land—and a boundary.
But maybe we could also see
The greater whole—the enormity.

Why not celebrate the globe,
Become a flag, and wear a robe
Of purest crimson? Convey to the world
We are all flags—and fly unfurled.
Then, while we honor one small place
Declare ourselves one, as a human race.

Julie Andrews

Hang Out the Flag

This is Flag Day.
Hang out the flags;
Watch them rise with the breeze
And droop when it sags.
Hang out the flags.

Hang them from short poles;
Hang them from long.
See their bright colors
Shimmering strong,
Drifting along.

Flags mean our Homeland,
Country we love.
Let them sparkle in sunshine
Proudly above,
Showing our love.

James S. Tippett

in daddy's arms

in daddy's arms i am tall
& close to the sun & warm
in daddy's arms

in daddy's arms
i can see over the fence out back
i can touch the bottom leaves of the big magnolia tree
in Cousin Sukie's yard
in daddy's arms

in my daddy's arms the moon is close
closer at night time when I can almost touch it
when it grins back at me from the wide twinkling skies

in daddy's arms i am tall
taller than Benny & my friends Ade & George
taller than Uncle Billy
& best of all
i am eye-ball-even-steven with my big brother Jamal

in my daddy's arms
i am strong & dark like him & laughing
happier than the circus clowns
with red painted grins
when daddy spins me round & round
& the whole world is crazy upside down
i am big and strong & proud like him
in daddy's arms
my daddy

Folami Abiade

For Father's Day

Here a little child I wait
Father dear, beside our gate.
When the sun is dropping low
And tired birds to branches go
That's the time I would not roam
Lest I miss your coming home.
And if God should chance to be
Looking from the sky at me
He would smile there in the blue
For He is Our Father, too.

Rachel Field

Experiment

Before you leave these portals
To meet less fortunate mortals,
There's just one final message
I would give to you.
You all have learned reliance
On the sacred teachings of science,
So I hope, through life, you never will decline
In spite of philistine
Defiance
To do what all good scientists do.

Experiment.
Make it your motto day and night.
Experiment
And it will lead you to the light.
The apple on the top of the tree
Is never too high to achieve,
So take an example from Eve,
Experiment.
Be curious,
Though interfering friends may frown.
Get furious
At each attempt to hold you down.
If this advice you always employ
The future can offer you infinite joy
And merriment.
Experiment
And you'll see.

Lyrics and music by Cole Porter

Remember

Remember the sky you were born under,
know each of the star's stories.
Remember the moon, know who she is.
Remember the sun's birth at dawn is the
strongest point of time. Remember sundown
and the giving away to night.
Remember your birth, how your mother struggled
to give you form and breath. You are evidence of
her life, and her mother's, and hers.
Remember your father. He is your life, also.
Remember the earth whose skin you are:
red earth, black earth, yellow earth, white earth
brown earth, we are earth.
Remember the plants, trees, animal life who all have their
tribes, their families, their histories, too. Talk to them,
listen to them. They are alive poems.
Remember the wind. Remember her voice. She knows the
origin of this universe.
Remember you are all people and that all people are you.
Remember you are the universe and this universe is you.
Remember all is in motion, is growing, is you.
Remember language comes from this.
Remember the dance language is, that life is.
Remember.

Joy Harjo

Midsummer Night

If you're in the woods on Midsummer Night,
  And the moon is full and clear,
Maybe you'll see some wonderful things
  Not very far from here.

If you find a circle of oak and beech,
  With carpet of moss between,
You must be sure to hide behind
  A twisted black-thorn screen.

Then if you're lucky and find the spot,
  And willing to wait a while,
Perhaps you'll see the fairies dance,
  After the fairy style.

All hands round in a fairy ring,
  And weaving in and out,
With never a sound to let one know
  The dancers are about.

Light as thistledown on the moss,
  With flickering firefly wands,
Acorn caps on their tiny heads,
  Mantles of green fern-fronds.

There in the silver summer night
  Round and round they swing,
Keeping time to the breeze that blows
  Over the fairy ring.

I haven't found just the right place yet,
  Or perhaps I left too soon,
And they only dance on Midsummer Night,
  In the light of a clear full moon.

But I mean to hunt through the oak and beech,
  I may find the ring by chance;
For I greatly want to be watching there
  Next time that the fairies dance.

Rupert S. Holland

July

To July

Here's to July,
Here's to July,
For the bird,
And the bee,
And the butterfly;
For the flowers
That blossom
For feasting the eye;
For skates, balls,
And jump ropes,
For swings that go high;
For rocketry
Fireworks that
Blaze in the sky,
Oh, here's to July!

Anonymous

Going Down Hill on a Bicycle
A Boy's Song

With lifted feet, hands still,
I am poised, and down the hill
Dart, with heedful mind;
The air goes by in a wind.

Swifter and yet more swift,
Till the heart with a mighty lift
Makes the lungs laugh, the throat cry:—
'O bird, see; see, bird, I fly.

'Is this, is this your joy?
O bird, then I, though a boy,
For a golden moment share
Your feathery life in air!'

Say, heart, is there aught like this
In a world that is full of bliss?
'Tis more than skating, bound
Steel-shod to the level ground.

Speed slackens now, I float
Awhile in my airy boat;
Till, when the wheels scarce crawl,
My feet to the treadles fall.

Alas, that the longest hill
Must end in a vale; but still,
Who climbs with toil, wheresoe'er,
Shall find wings waiting there.

Henry Charles Beeching

Natural History

The spider, dropping down from twig,
Unwinds a thread of her devising:
A thin, premeditated rig
To use in rising.

And all that journey down through space,
In cool descent, and loyal-hearted,
She builds a ladder to the place
From which she started.

Thus I, gone forth, as spiders do,
In spider's web a truth discerning,
Attach one silken strand to you
For my returning.

E. B. White

The Frog Chorus

Come to the marsh when the fireflies glisten,
Come to the bank and stop and listen;
  Big bass frog and little bass frog,
  Some in the reeds and some on a log,
Singing away in the big frog chorus,
Singing away in the pond before us.

Scores and scores of frogs in rows—
How many singers nobody knows—
  Shrill little fellow and big-voiced one,
  Keeping so quiet till set of sun,
And then, when stars begin to peep,
Starting their basso and tenor and cheep.

Slowly the moon rides up in the sky,
Dimming the light of the marsh firefly;
  Butterflies long have gone to rest,
  Birds are safe in their little nest,
But hour after hour the frogs will sing,
For they like that better than anything.

It isn't a regular rousing chorus,
That in the reeds and bog before us—
  Croak, croak, croak, the big ones bellow,
  Cheep, cheep, cheep, goes the little fellow,
And never stopping to change their song,
The chorus of frogs sings all night long.

Rupert S. Holland

Equestrienne

See, they are clearing the sawdust course
For the girl in pink on the milk-white horse.
Her spangles twinkle; his pale flanks shine,
Every hair of his tail is fine
And bright as a comet's; his mane blows free
And she points a toe and bends a knee,
The while his hoofbeats fall like rain
Over and over and over again.
And nothing that moves on land or sea
Will seem so beautiful to me
As the girl in pink on the milk-white horse
Cantering over the sawdust course.

Rachel Field

Sand House

I built a house
 One afternoon
With bucket, cup
 And tablespoon,

Then scooped a shovel-
 ful of shore
On top to add
 The second floor.

But when the fingers
 Of the sea
Reached up and waved
 A wave to me,

It tumbled down
 Like dominoes
And disappeared
 Between my toes.

J. Patrick Lewis

Reading: Summer

Summer is with it,
    she's wild,
    she likes
    bare legs and cutoffs
    and camping
    and hikes;
    she dives in deep water,
    she wades in a stream,
    she guzzles cold drinks
    and she drowns in ice cream;
    she runs barefoot,
    she picnics,
    she fishes,
    digs bait,
    she pitches a tent
    and she stays up too late
    while she counts out the stars,
    swats mosquitoes and flies,
    hears crickets,
    smells pine trees,
    spies night-creature eyes;
    she rides bareback,
    goes sailing,
    plays tennis,
    climbs trees;
    she soaks in the sunshine;
    she gulps in a breeze;
    she tastes the warm air
    on the end of her tongue,

and she falls asleep
reading
alone
in the sun.

Myra Cohn Livingston

A Boy's Summer

With a line and hook
By a babbling brook,
The fisherman's sport we ply;
And list the song
of the feathered throng
That flits in the branches nigh.
At last we strip
For a quiet dip;
Ah, that is the best of joy.
For this I say
On a summer's day,
What's so fine as being a boy?
Ha, Ha!

Paul Laurence Dunbar

A Boy and His Dad

A boy and his dad on a fishing-trip—
There is a glorious fellowship!
Father and son and the open sky
And the white clouds lazily drifting by,
And the laughing stream as it runs along
With the clicking reel like a martial song,
And the father teaching the youngster gay
How to land a fish in the sportsman's way.

I fancy I hear them talking there
In an open boat, and the speech is fair.
And the boy is learning the ways of men
From the finest man in his youthful ken.
Kings, to the youngster, cannot compare
With the gentle father who's with him there.
And the greatest mind of the human race
Not for one minute could take his place.

Which is happier, man or boy?
The soul of the father is steeped in joy,
For he's finding out, to his heart's delight,
That his son is fit for the future fight.
He is learning the glorious depths of him,
And the thoughts he thinks and his every whim;
And he shall discover, when night comes on,
How close he has grown to his little son.

A boy and his dad on a fishing-trip—
Builders of life's companionship!
Oh, I envy them, as I see them there
Under the sky in the open air,
For out of the old, old long-ago
Come the summer days that I used to know,
When I learned life's truths from my father's lips
As I shared the joy of his fishing-trips.

Edgar A. Guest

103

Ramadan Has Begun

Ramadan has begun,
    So don't wake the sun
        Until after our *suhur*[1] is served.
Not a sip nor a bite
    Till the day turns to night
        And the prayers of our faith are observed.
Ramadan will end soon
    With the new crescent moon,
        So we give to the ones who have least.
Happy neighbors prepare
    Meats and sweets they will share
        At the fast-breaking festival feast!

Jenny Whitehead

[1] A meal eaten early in the morning before daily
Ramadan fasting begins

I Will Go With My Father A-Ploughing

I will go with my father a-ploughing
To the green field by the sea,
And the rooks and crows and sea-gulls
Will come flocking after me.
I will sing to the patient horses,
With the lark in the white of the air,
And my father will sing the plough-song
That blesses the cleaving share.

I will go with my father a-sowing
To the red field by the sea,
And the rooks and the gulls and the starlings
Will come flocking after me.
I will sing to the striding sowers
With the finch on the greening sloe,
And my father will sing the seed-song
That only the wise men know.

I will go with my father a-reaping
To the brown field by the sea,
And the geese and the crows and the children
Will come flocking after me.
I will sing to the tan-faced reapers,
With the wren in the heat of the sun,
And my father will sing the scythe-song
That joys for the harvest done.

Joseph Campbell

Nocturne for Late Summer

Hot   languid
the still days roll over us
but the dark comes earlier
now.

In the rubble near the playground
fence
one cricket tunes
his fiddle.   Begins

Under a sky the color of opals
he is playing *allegro*.
Adding thirty-seven
he heats up the night to ninety
degrees.

Soon the winds will swing
north. Somewhere a yellow leaf
edged with red
already hides in green branches.

Crickets will play
their *andante* cadenza
for fifteen bars add thirty-seven

The leaf
    will
       fall...

              Barbara Juster Esbensen

Note: Did you know that by counting the number of chirps a cricket makes in a fifteen-second period, then adding thirty-seven, you can get a fair approximation of the temperature in degrees Fahrenheit?

What Shall I Pack in the Box Marked "Summer"?

A handful of wind that I caught with a kite
A firefly's flame in the dark of the night
The green grass of June that I tasted with toes
The flowers I knew from the tip of my nose
The clink of the ice cubes in pink lemonade
The Fourth of July Independence parade!
The sizzle of hot dogs, the fizzle of Coke
Some pickles and mustard and barbecue smoke
The print of my fist in the palm of my mitt.
As I watched for the batter to strike out or hit
The splash of the water, the top-to-toe cool
Of a stretch-and-kick trip through a blue swimming pool
The tangle of night songs that slipped through my screen
Of crickets and insects too small to be seen
The seed pods that formed on the flowers to say
That summer was packing her treasures away.

Bobbi Katz

Fall

*S*eptember is one of the best-kept secrets on the East End of Long Island, where we both live. As Helen Hunt Jackson says, it's "summer's best of weather, and autumn's best of cheer." And autumn is *filled* with cheer! There's the unmistakable scent of chrysanthemums; apple, cranberry, and pumpkin picking; riotous colors everywhere; huge shiny tractors—marvels of power and locomotion—trundling along our lanes and harvesting potatoes in the fields.

Grandparents' Day is my delight! I've had a lot of nicknames, but "Granny Jools" is without a doubt my favorite.

Of course, it's also back-to-school time. Barbara Juster Esbensen captures so well the bittersweet feelings of that first day. Grandparents' Day is *my* delight! I've had a lot of nicknames, but "Granny Jools" is without a doubt my favorite.

One of the best times of year with my grandchildren is Halloween. I'm always tickled by their costume choices, usually indicative of their personalities. We've had a vampire, a Power Ranger, a princess, a cowboy, and a wedge of cheese all in one day! There is a tradition in our village known as the Ragamuffin Parade, when all the children in the area march up Main Street in costume as a preview of the holiday ahead. The following week, they follow the "Pumpkin Trail" and trick-or-treat at every store in town. All are welcome, and hundreds of children are free to roam safely, since traffic is stopped for the afternoon in honor of this festive occasion. People come from far and near, neighbors and friends meet and greet and stand in clusters, watching the explosion of creativity all around. Even the dogs are in costume!

Less than a month later, the abundance of Thanksgiving is upon us. The wonderful Jack Prelutsky obviously loves this holiday, as he's written so much on the subject—and seems to enjoy its culinary delights as much as we do! The celebration is that much more special because it's about being grateful for gifts we already have.

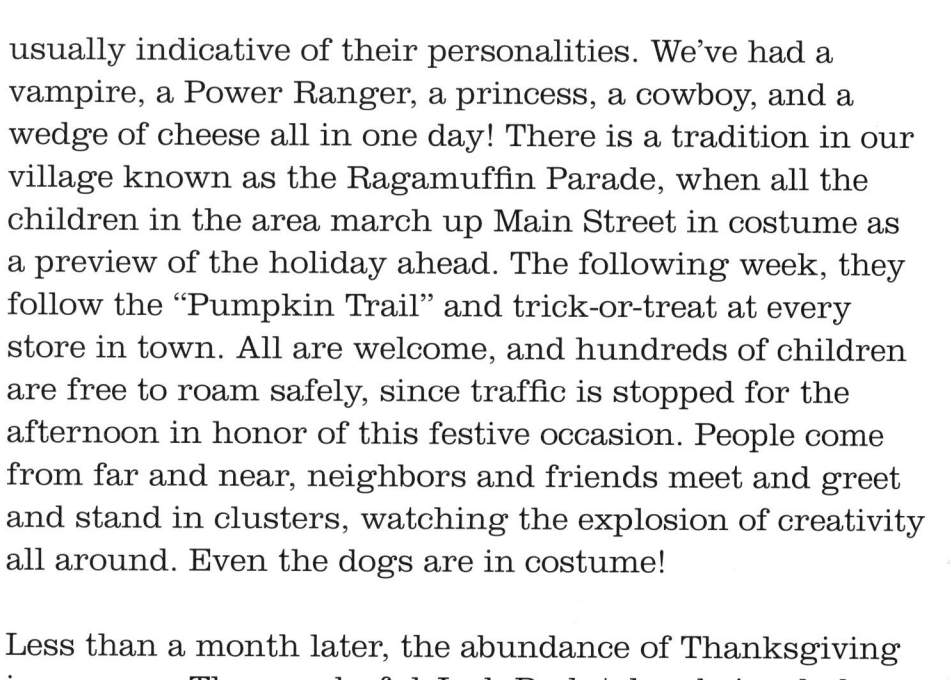

September

The golden-rod is yellow;
  The corn is turning brown;
The trees in apple orchards
  With fruit are bending down.

The gentian's bluest fringes
  Are curling in the sun;
In dusty pods the milkweed
  Its hidden silk has spun.

The sedges flaunt their harvest,
  In every meadow nook;
And asters by the brook-side
  Make asters in the brook.

From dewy lanes at morning
  The grapes' sweet odors rise;
At noon the roads all flutter
  With yellow butterflies.

By all these lovely tokens
  September days are here,
With summer's best of weather,
  And autumn's best of cheer.

But none of all this beauty
  Which floods the earth and air
Is unto me the secret
  Which makes September fair.

'T is a thing which I remember;
  To name it thrills me yet:
One day of one September
  I never can forget.

Helen Hunt Jackson

First Day of School

No more barefoot
days.
My feet are clean,
my new socks come up
to my knees.
Inside the school-shoes
my toes are stiff
and afraid of the dark.

The sidewalk is bright
with sun
and holds the old heat
of August
in the cracks.
We can't feel its rough
skin
through our soles now
and it really doesn't know us
anymore.

Barbara Juster Esbensen

Good Hot Dogs
(for Kiki)

Fifty cents apiece
To eat our lunch
We'd run
Straight from school
Instead of home
Two blocks
Then the store
That smelled like steam
You ordered
Because you had the money
Two hot dogs and two pops for here
Everything on the hot dogs
Except pickle lily
Dash those hot dogs
Into buns and splash on
All that good stuff
Yellow mustard and onions
And french fries piled on top all
Rolled up in a piece of wax
Paper for us to hold hot
In our hands
Quarters on the counter
Sit down
Good hot dogs
We'd eat
Fast till there was nothing left
But salt and poppy seeds even
The little burnt tips
Of french fries
We'd eat
You humming
And me swinging my legs

Sandra Cisneros

Homework

Homework sits on top of Sunday, squashing Sunday flat.
Homework has the smell of Monday, homework's very fat.
Heavy books and piles of paper, answers I don't know.
Sunday evening's almost finished, now I'm going to go
Do my homework in the kitchen. Maybe just a snack,
Then I'll sit right down and start as soon as I run back
For some chocolate sandwich cookies. Then I'll really do
All that homework in a minute. First I'll see what new
Show they've got on television in the living room.
Everybody's laughing there, but misery and gloom
And a full refrigerator are where I am at.
I'll just have another sandwich. Homework's very fat.

Russell Hoban

grandmother

if i were to see
her shape from a mile away
i'd know so quickly
that it would be her.
the purple scarf
and the plastic
shopping bag.
if i felt
hands on my head
i'd know that those
were her hands
warm and damp
with the smell
of roots.
if i heard
a voice
coming from
a rock
i'd know
and her words
would flow inside me
like the light
of someone
stirring ashes
from a sleeping fire
at night.

Ray A. Young Bear

Some Things About Grandpas

Grandfathers *watch* you
They always have time
To see you play baseball
Or jump rope or climb.
Grandpas make whistles
And kites that go high
And boats for your bathtub
And planes that can fly.

Grandfathers *know* things
Like what is a star
And why does it thunder
And how far is far
And grandpas tell stories
With you on their knee
(And there's no other place
That it's nicer to be).

Alice Low

Rosh ha-Shanah Eve

Stale moon, climb down.
Clear the sky.
Get out of town.
Good-bye.

Fresh moon, arise.
Throw a glow.
Shine a surprise.
Hello

New Year, amen.
Now we begin:
Teach me to be a new me.

Harry Philip

How to Get Through the Memorial Service

If restless, let little words
come to your aid:
drop an "e" into "fast"
and enjoy the sudden feast.
Double the "o" in God.
That's good.
Count the burnt-out bulbs
drooping from the high ceiling.
Each dark bulb is a teardrop
among the living lights.

If restless still,
peek at your mother.
See the teardrops wet her cheek
like melted snow.
Someone she softly misses:
her big sister, your aunt,
who cried these very prayers
last Yom Kippur.
Now touch your mother's hand.
Let her feel your light.

Richard J. Margolis

Columbus

Once upon a time there was an Italian,
And some people thought he was a rapscallion,
But he wasn't offended,
Because other people thought he was splendid,
And he said the world was round,
And everybody made an uncomplimentary sound,
But his only reply was Pooh,
He replied, Isn't this fourteen ninety-two?
It's time for me to discover America if I know my chronology,
And if I discover America you owe me an apology,
So he went and tried to borrow some money from Ferdinand
But Ferdinand said America was a bird in the bush and he'd rather
        have a berdinand,
But Columbus' brain was fertile, it wasn't arid,
And he remembered that Ferdinand was married,
And he thought, there is no wife like a misunderstood one,
Because her husband thinks something is a terrible idea she is
        bound to think it a good one,
So he perfumed his handkerchief with bay rum and citronella,
And he went to see Isabella,
And he looked wonderful but he had never felt sillier,

And she said, I can't place the face but the aroma is familiar,
And Columbus didn't say a word,
All he said was, I am Columbus, the fifteenth-century
    Admiral Byrd,
And just as he thought, her disposition was very malleable,
And she said, Here are my jewels, and she wasn't penurious
    like Cornelia the mother of the Gracchi, she wasn't
    referring to her children, no, she was referring to her
    jewels, which were very very valuable,
So Columbus said, somebody show me the sunset and
    somebody did and he set sail for it,
And he discovered America and they put him in jail for it,
And the fetters gave him welts,
And they named America after somebody else,
So the sad fate of Columbus ought to be pointed out to every
    child and every voter,
Because it has a very important moral, which is, Don't be a
    discoverer, be a promoter.

Ogden Nash

To Autumn

Season of mists and mellow fruitfulness,
 Close bosom-friend of the maturing sun;
Conspiring with him how to load and bless
 With fruit the vines that round the thatch-eves run;
To bend with apples the moss'd cottage-trees,
 And fill all fruit with ripeness to the core;
  To swell the gourd, and plump the hazel shells
 With a sweet kernel; to set budding more,
And still more, later flowers for the bees,
Until they think warm days will never cease,
  For Summer has o'er-brimm'd their clammy cells.

Who hath not seen thee oft amid thy store?
 Sometimes whoever seeks abroad may find
Thee sitting careless on a granary floor,
 Thy hair soft-lifted by the winnowing wind;
Or on a half-reap'd furrow sound asleep,
 Drows'd with the fume of poppies, while thy hook
  Spares the next swath and all its twined flowers:
And sometimes like a gleaner thou dost keep
 Steady thy laden head across a brook;
 Or by a cyder-press, with patient look,
  Thou watchest the last oozings hours by hours.

Where are the songs of Spring? Ay, where are they?
 Think not of them, thou hast thy music too,—
While barred clouds bloom the soft-dying day,
 And touch the stubble-plains with rosy hue;
Then in a wailful choir the small gnats mourn
 Among the river sallows, borne aloft
  Or sinking as the light wind lives or dies;
And full-grown lambs loud bleat from hilly bourn;
 Hedge-crickets sing; and now with treble soft
 The red-breast whistles from a garden-croft;
  And gathering swallows twitter in the skies.

John Keats

Apple Song

The apples are seasoned
And ripe and sound.
Gently they fall
On the yellow ground.

The apples are stored
In the dusky bin
Where hardly a glimmer
Of light creeps in.

In the firelit, winter
Nights, they'll be
The clear sweet taste
Of a summer tree!

Frances Frost

126

Autumn

The morns are meeker than they were,
The nuts are getting brown;
The berry's cheek is plumper,
The rose is out of town.

The maple wears a gayer scarf,
The field a scarlet gown.
Lest I should be old-fashioned,
I'll put a trinket on.

Emily Dickinson

The Wind in a Frolic

The wind one morning sprung up from sleep,
Saying, 'Now for a frolic! now for a leap!
Now for a mad-cap, galloping chase!
I'll make a commotion in every place!'
So it swept with a bustle right through a great town,
Creaking the signs, and scattering down
Shutters; and whisking, with merciless squalls,
Old women's bonnets and gingerbread stalls.
There never was heard a much lustier shout,
As the apples and oranges trundled about;
And the urchins, that stand with their thievish eyes
For ever on watch, ran off each with a prize.

Then away to the field it went blustering and humming,
And the cattle all wondered whatever was coming;
It plucked by their tails the grave, matronly cows,
And tossed the colts' manes all about their brows,
Till, offended at such a familiar salute,
They all turned their backs, and stood sullenly mute.
So on it went, capering and playing its pranks:
Whistling with reeds on the broad river's banks;
Puffing the birds as they sat on the spray,
Or the traveller grave on the king's highway.
It was not too nice to hustle the bags
Of the beggar, and flutter his dirty rags;
'Twas so bold, that it feared not to play its joke
With the doctor's wig, or the gentleman's cloak.
Through the forest it roared, and cried gaily, 'Now,
You sturdy old oaks, I'll make you bow!'

And it made them bow without more ado,
Or it cracked their great branches through and through.

Then it rushed like a monster on cottage and farm,
Striking their dwellers with sudden alarm;
And they ran out like bees in a midsummer swarm.
There were dames with their 'kerchiefs tied over their caps,
To see if their poultry were free from mishaps;
The turkeys they gobbled, the geese screamed aloud,
And the hens crept to roost in a terrified crowd;
There was rearing of ladders, and logs laying on
Where the thatch from the roof threatened soon to be gone.

But the wind had passed on, and had met in a lane,
With a schoolboy, who panted and struggled in vain;
For it tossed him, and twirled him, then passed, and he stood,
With his hat in a pool, and his shoe in the mud.

But away went the wind in its holiday glee;
And now it was far on the billowy sea,
And the lordly ships felt its staggering blow,
And the little boats darted to and fro.
But lo! it was night, and it sank to rest,
On the sea-bird's rock, in the gleaming west,
Laughing to think, in its fearful fun,
How little of mischief it had done.

William Howitt
(Abridged version)

Hallowe'en

On Hallowe'en the witches fly
Astride of broom-sticks in the sky,
And goblins romp and run and race
To see the witches fly through space;
For all the sprites of earth and air
Slip out on Hallowe'en and fare
Abroad to dance until the sun
Makes witches, goblins, fairies run.

Upon the garden wall we place
A candle-lighted pumpkin face,
Astride of brooms, in sheets of white,
We gallop in the clear moonlight;
Then when we've had enough of elves,
We're glad to be just our own selves,
And eat as much as we are able
Of nuts and apples on the table.

We'd rather have the witches fly
On Hallowe'en across the sky;
And gladly let the goblins roam,
While we eat supper in our home.

Rupert S. Holland

Skeletons

Is it the
Curve of their
Breezy ribs, the
Crook of their
Elegant fingers,

Their eyeless
Eyes, so wide
And wise,
Their silent
Ivory laughter,

The frisk and
Prance of their
Skittering dance
With never a
Pause for breath,

That fill us
With such
Delicious delight,
While scaring us
Half to death?

Valerie Worth

Pumpkin

After its lid
Is cut, the slick
Seeds and stuck
Wet strings
Scooped out,
Walls scraped
Dry and white,
Face carved, candle
Fixed and lit,

Light creeps
Into the thick
Rind: giving
That dead orange
Vegetable skull
Warm skin, making
A live head
To hold its
Sharp gold grin.

Valerie Worth

131

November

The stripped and shapely
    Maple grieves
The loss of her
    Departed leaves.

The ground is hard,
    As hard as stone.
The year is old,
    The birds are flown.

And yet the world,
    Nevertheless,
Displays a certain
    Loveliness—

The beauty of
    The bone. Tall God
Must see our souls
    This way, and nod.

Give thanks: we do,
    Each in his place
Around the table
    During grace.

John Updike

Autumn Fires

In the other gardens
    And all up the vale,
From the autumn bonfires
    See the smoke trail!

Pleasant summer over
    And all the summer flowers,
The red fire blazes,
    The grey smoke towers.

Sing a song of seasons!
    Something bright in all!
Flowers in the summer,
    Fires in the fall!

Robert Louis Stevenson

The First Thanksgiving

When the Pilgrims
first gathered together to share
with their Indian friends
in the mild autumn air,
they lifted the voices
in jubilant praise
for the bread on the table,
the berries and maize,
for field and for forest,
for turkey and deer,
for the bountiful crops
they were blessed with that year.
They were thankful for these
as they feasted away,
and as they were thankful,
we're thankful today.

Jack Prelutsky

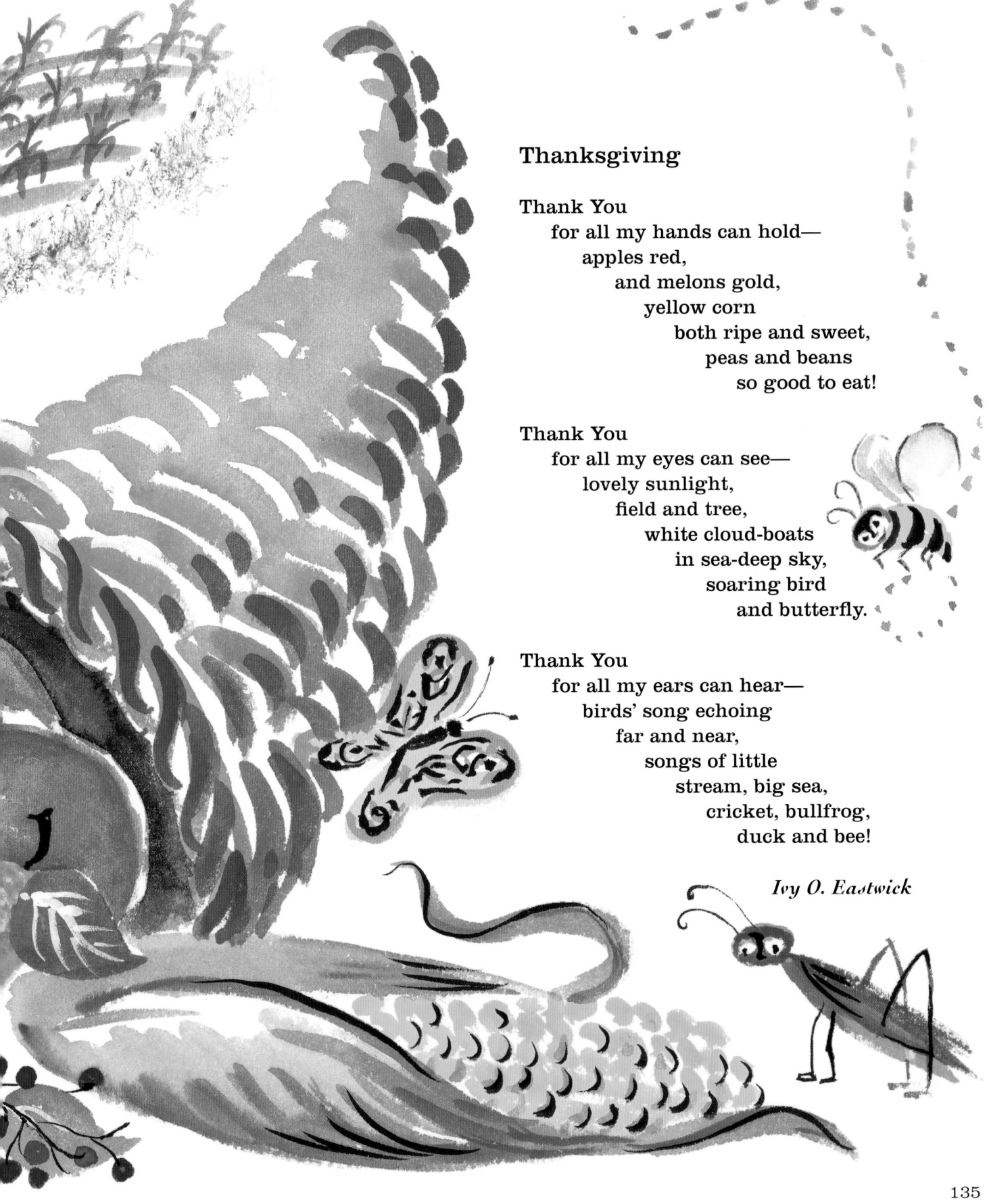

Thanksgiving

Thank You
for all my hands can hold—
apples red,
and melons gold,
yellow corn
both ripe and sweet,
peas and beans
so good to eat!

Thank You
for all my eyes can see—
lovely sunlight,
field and tree,
white cloud-boats
in sea-deep sky,
soaring bird
and butterfly.

Thank You
for all my ears can hear—
birds' song echoing
far and near,
songs of little
stream, big sea,
cricket, bullfrog,
duck and bee!

Ivy O. Eastwick

135

Father, We Thank Thee

For flowers that bloom about our feet,
    Father, we thank Thee,
For tender grass so fresh and sweet,
    Father, we thank Thee,
For the song of bird and hum of bee,
For all things fair we hear or see,
Father in heaven, we thank Thee.

For blue of stream and blue of sky,
    Father, we thank Thee,
For pleasant shade of branches high,
    Father, we thank Thee,
For fragrant air and cooling breeze,
For beauty of the blooming trees,
Father in heaven, we thank Thee.

For this new morning with its light,
    Father, we thank Thee,
For rest and shelter of the night,
    Father, we thank Thee,
For health and food, for love and friends,
For everything Thy goodness sends,
Father in heaven, we thank Thee.

Ralph Waldo Emerson

Rhapsody

I am glad daylong for the gift of song,
For time and change and sorrow;
For the sunset wings and the world-end things
Which hang on the edge of tomorrow.
I am glad for my heart whose gates apart
Are the entrance-place of wonders,
Where dreams come in from the rush and din
Like sheep from the rains and thunders.

William Stanley Braithwaite

I Ate Too Much

I ate too much turkey,
I ate too much corn,
I ate too much pudding and pie,
I'm stuffed up with muffins
and much too much stuffin',
I'm probably going to die.
I piled up my plate
and I ate and I ate,
but I wish I had known when to stop,
for I'm so crammed with yams,
sauces, gravies, and jams
that my buttons are starting to pop.
I'm full of tomatoes
and french fried potatoes,
my stomach is swollen and sore,
but there's still some dessert,
so I guess it won't hurt
if I eat just a little bit more.

Jack Prelutsky

Jack Frost

Someone painted pictures on my
Window pane last night—
Willow trees with trailing boughs
And flowers—frosty white
And lovely crystal butterflies;
But when the morning sun
Touched them with its golden beams,
They vanished one by one!

Helen Bayley Davis

December Lights

*I*t's no accident that so many of the choices for this section celebrate light—for everything seems to be graced with it at this time of year. Whether it be village illuminations, candles twinkling in windows, menorahs or kinaras, glowing hearths, or sparkling Christmas trees with bright stars on top reminding us of an even brighter star in the East…it all reflects the extra light that's in our hearts.

In our village, the festivities begin with a visit from Santa, who arrives on a red fire truck. A mailbox for letters to the North Pole is installed on the corner of Main Street, and shop windows, rooflines, church spires, and windmills are outlined with holiday lights. More often than not we're fortunate to have a snowfall.

I have always been touched by the music of Christmas—not necessarily the average jingle, but the magic of voices raised in praise and celebration, be they in a church or temple, caroling door-to-door, or gathered around the family fireside. Perhaps my favorite carol is "A Christmas Carol." Christina Rosetti's words perfectly capture a humble bystander's experience of that one holy night. Then, of course, there are the bells—church bells, sleigh bells, cowbells, doorbells…even bell choirs!

Perhaps no other time of year is quite so rich with tradition, and there are a number that we enjoy: Advent calendars, the making of gingerbread houses and cookies, tree decorating, letters to Santa, the hanging of stockings on the mantel. On Christmas Eve, Emma and her children prepare a "Nativity tray" with nuts, fruits, berries and seeds, raw vegetables, and even a bone or two and place it in their front garden as an offering to any stray animals or birds that might pass by that evening.

My mother began a tradition that I continue and have passed on to my children. We save one small present—we call it a tree gift—for each member of the family, and it is hidden in the tree until Christmas night. It is the last event of the day, long after all the other gifts have been opened, meals have been enjoyed, visits have been paid, walks have been taken. We enjoy a last cup of tea, cider, or spiced wine by the fire, and, as one, we each open that last tiny offering.

I have always been touched by the music of Christmas—not necessarily the average jingle, but the magic of voices raised in praise and celebration...

New Year's Eve is ripe with tradition as well. The potentially endless wait until midnight is filled with games like charades, the watching of local fireworks, and a particular pastime that gives us much pleasure—the Three-Minute Game. Everyone pulls a subject out of a hat and, armed with nothing more than pencil and paper, free-associates for three minutes about whatever comes to mind. Needless to say, this is a wonderful way to capture a moment in time, and I've bound many a book containing those family mementoes.

Of course, there are also resolutions to be made. Emma's family has a keepsake box, which is decorated each year with new family photos to make an ever-growing collage. Inside, each person has his or her own small notebook in which this year's resolutions are dutifully entered, and last year's are read aloud and assessed.

The New Year is a time to reflect on the past, celebrate the future, and appreciate the moment all at the same time. Wish we could hold that thought year-round!

Latke Time

Grate the potatoes gently,
chop some onions, too.
It's time to make some latkes,
a heaping plate for you!

Heat the griddle slowly,
pour the oil in,
fry up forty latkes,
let the feast begin!

The oil's a reminder
of a story long ago
when lamps in a temple
continued to glow

longer than they should have.
Eight days of light!
We're celebrating Hanukkah
with latkes tonight!

Michele Krueger

A Sacred Place
Traditional Jewish Prayer

How wonderful, O Lord, are the works of your hands!
The heavens declare Your glory,
the arch of sky displays Your handiwork.
In Your love You have given us the power
to behold the beauty of Your world
robed in all its splendor.
The sun and the stars, the valleys and hills,
the rivers and lakes all disclose Your presence.
The roaring breakers of the sea tell of Your awesome might,
the beasts of the field and the birds of the air
bespeak Your wondrous will.
In Your goodness You have made us able to hear
the music of the world. The voices of loved ones
reveal to us that You are in our midst.
A divine voice sings through all creation.

Anonymous

For Christmas

Now not a window small or big
But wears a wreath or holly sprig;
Nor any shop too poor to show
Its spray of pine or mistletoe.
Now city airs are spicy-sweet
With Christmas trees along each street,
Green spruce and fir whose boughs will hold
Their tinseled balls and fruits of gold.
Now postmen pass in threes and fours
Like bent, blue-coated Santa Claus.
Now people hurry to and fro
With little girls and boys in tow,
And not a child but keeps some trace
Of Christmas secrets in his face.

Rachel Field

Christmas

This year
Let's remember what it's for.
Be aware a little more.
Let us give in thought and deed and word.
And share.
And show that we care.
This year.

This year
Let's remember what it's all about.
Let's not shout
And babble about happiness and so on.
Unless we mean it.
Let's not give in excess
And somehow give less
Of ourselves.
This year.

This year
Let us <u>quietly</u> wish each other well.
And meaningfully tell
Our hopes and fears.
Let us make the feelings right.
And build upon them day and night
So that next year in retrospect
It will have seemed like a beginning.
   This year.

Julie Andrews

149

little tree

little tree
little silent Christmas tree
you are so little
you are more like a flower

who found you in the green forest
and were you very sorry to come away?
see   i will comfort you
because you smell so sweetly

i will kiss your cool bark
and hug you safe and tight
just as your mother would,
only don't be afraid

look   the spangles
that sleep all the year in a dark box
dreaming of being taken out and allowed to shine,
the balls the chains red and gold the fluffy threads,

put up your little arms
and i'll give them all to you to hold
every finger shall have its ring
and there won't be a single place dark or unhappy

then when you're quite dressed
you'll stand in the window for everyone to see
and how they'll stare!
oh but you'll be very proud

and my little sister and i will take hands
and looking up at our beautiful tree
we'll dance and sing
"Noel Noel"

e. e. cummings

Christmas Goes to Sea

I saw a fishing boat steer by,
Blunt-prowed beneath the winter sky,
    As Christmas dusk was falling.

The hull was crusted dark with spray,
The waters all about spread gray,
    And sea gulls followed calling.

But to the masthead gallantly
Was lashed a little Christmas tree,
    A green-armed pledge of pine.

No bright festoons or gifts it bore,
And yet those empty boughs held more
    Than tinsel for a sign.

So fair a sight it was to see—
That small, seafaring Christmas tree
    High amid shroud and spar.

And all night long I thought of it
Salt-drenched, wind-buffeted, and lit
    By Bethlehem's bright star.

Rachel Field

How Do You Get to Be Santa?

How do you get to be Santa?
It must be the greatest career...
to spend so much time having fun in the snow
and work only one month a year!

The rest of the time you could frolic,
or lounge in your hammock and think,
or revel awhile on a tropical isle
to ensure that your cheeks remain pink.

But what would you need to be Santa?
You'd need to appreciate red,
be blessed with great girth,
a good map of the earth,
and a license to pilot a sled.

What qualifications would serve you the best
for winning this special position?
Perhaps there's some kind of a "Ho, ho, ho" test
or a "belly like jelly" audition?

What else do you think's a credential
for winning this coveted role?
A fondness for elves is essential,
plus a residence at the North Pole.

You'd have to be hip to the trendiest toys,
resistant to holiday stress,
and ease down a chimney without making noise
or leaving soot footprints or mess.

Grinches and Scrooges should never apply,
nor anyone sullen or sour.
And give it a miss if you're nervous to fly,
or want to be paid by the hour.

It's possible you'd feel uneasy
distributing gifts with such haste.
And maybe you'd get kind of queasy
from all of the cookies you'd taste?

If holidays are your essential days off,
that might be quite hard to achieve...
for even if sick with a cold or a cough
you'd still have to work Christmas Eve.

Your sleigh seat might well not be heated.
The weather could well be unkind.
And why would you want to be seated
downwind of a reindeer's behind?

So think very carefully if they should ask you
to take on this noble endeavor...
for maybe you're better off leaving the task to
the fellow who's done it forever!

Emma Walton Hamilton

The Holy Boy

Lowly, laid in a manger,
With oxen brooding nigh,
The Heav'nly Babe is lying,
His Maiden Mother by.
Lo! the wayfaring sages,
Who journey'd far through the wild,
Now worship, silent, adoring,
The Boy, the Heav'nly Child
The Heav'nly Child!

Leave your work and your playtime,
And kneel in homage and prayer,
The Prince of Love is smiling
Asleep in His cradle there!
Bend your heart to the wonder,
The Birth, the Mystery mild,
And worship, silent, adoring,
The Boy, the Heav'nly Child
The Heav'nly Child!

Dim the light of the lantern,
And bare the mean abode,
Yet gold and myrrh and incense
Proclaim the Son of God.
Lowly, laid in a manger
By Virgin undefiled,
Come worship, silent, adoring,
The Boy, the Heav'nly Child
The Heav'nly Child!

Lyrics by Herbert S. Brown
Music by John Ireland

Kid Stuff

The wise guys
tell me
that Christmas
is Kid Stuff...
Maybe they've got
something there—
Two thousand years ago
three wise guys
chased a star
across a continent
to bring
frankincense and myrrh
to a Kid
born in a manger
with an idea in his head...

And as the bombs
crash
all over the world
today
the real wise guys
know
that we've all
got to go chasing stars
again
in the hope
that we can get back
some of that
Kid Stuff
born two thousand years ago.

Frank Horne

The Waiting Game

Nuts and marbles in the toe,
An orange in the heel,
A Christmas stocking in the dark
Is wonderful to feel.

Shadowy, bulging length of leg
That crackles when you clutch,
A Christmas stocking in the dark
Is marvelous to touch.

You lie back on your pillow
But that shape's still hanging there.
A Christmas stocking in the dark
Is very hard to bear,

So try to get to sleep again
And chase the hours away.
A Christmas stocking in the dark
Must wait for Christmas Day.

John Mole

New Year's Eve

We got a broom (like Father said)
And just before we went to bed

We opened up the cold back door
And swept the old year out before

We ran to let the New Year in
The front, and told him to begin

And blew our horns and gave a shout
To see the old year running out.

Myra Cohn Livingston

Other Celebrations and Special Occasions

*T*here's something to celebrate every week of the year—even if it's just the arrival of the weekend. For some, it's the Sabbath or Shabbat; for others it's a welcome break from work or school. For us, the weekend is also an occasion for the best breakfast of the week!

Opportunities for celebration abound throughout our lives, and the miracle is that poets use the power of words to touch the very core of our being and make us weep or laugh in recognition.

Cole Porter's "Sunday Morning Breakfast Time" might well be our family anthem, were it not for the fact that he omits our personal favorite—pancakes! Sundays are precious family time for us, from pancake breakfast to roast dinner with all the trimmings, and as many children or grandchildren as are available. Quite often, I have as many as sixteen for dinner on Sunday nights—and that's just family!

Of course, birthdays are always cause for celebration. We were especially tickled to find Amy Krouse Rosenthal's "Half Birthday" since we often smile about the fact that when Emma was a little girl, she announced to a family friend that it was her birthday. Surprised, our friend said, "My goodness! How old are you?" Emma solemnly and sweetly replied, "I'm three and a half."

Poetry becomes a cherished gift when used to mark an important transition or commemorate a rite of passage. As a mother and a grandmother, I've witnessed more of these life-changing moments than I can count—from the miracle of birth to first days of school, double-digit birthdays, bar and bat mitzvahs, and sweet sixteens, as well as earning driver's licenses and the ability to vote, going off to college, graduating with that special degree, getting married, landing the first big job or promotion, becoming a parent for the first time....The list goes on and on.

Opportunities for celebration abound throughout our lives, and the miracle is that poets use the power of words to touch the very core of our being and make us weep or laugh in recognition.

And so, like a year, we come full circle and reflect back on the words of Henry Wadsworth Longfellow with which this book began and must now end:

> "Such songs have power to quiet
>   The restless pulse of care,
> And come like the benediction
>   That follows after prayer.
>
> Then read from the treasured volume
>   The poem of thy choice,
> And lend to the rhyme of the poet
>   The beauty of thy voice."

Sabbath Bells

Ive often on a sabbath day
Where pastoral quiet dwells
Lay down among the new mown hay
To listen distant bells
That beautifully flung the sound
Upon the quiet wind
While beans in blossom breathed around
A fragrance oer the mind

A fragrance and a joy beside
That never wears away
The very air seems deified
Upon a sabbath day
So beautiful the flitting wrack
Slow pausing from the eye
Earths music seemed to call them back
Calm settled in the sky

And I have listened till I felt
A feeling not in words
A love that rudest moods would melt
When those sweet sounds was heard
A melancholly joy at rest
A pleasurable pain
A love a rapture of the breast
That nothing will explain

A dream of beauty that displays
Imaginary joys
That all the world in all its ways
Finds not to realize
All idly stretched upon the hay
The wind flirt fanning bye
How soft how sweetly swept away
The music of the sky

The ear it lost and caught the sound
Swelled beautifully on
A fitful melody around
Of sweetness heard and gone
I felt such thoughts I yearned to sing
The humming airs delight
That seemed to move the swallows wing
Into a wilder flight

The butterflye in wings of brown
Would find me where I lay
Fluttering and bobbing up and down
And settling on the hay
The waving blossoms seemed to throw
Their fragrance to the sound
While up and down and loud and low
The bells were ringing round

John Clare

Havdalah

"A good week," we sing
at the end of Shabbat.

"A week as bright as
candlelight, as
sweet as spice
and sweeter than wine!

"A good week!" we sing
as we light the candles
sniff the spice box
and lifting the wine cup
take a sip.

Can you see the light
dancing on your fingertips?

Can you feel inside
another week
ready to begin?

Carol Adler

Sunday Morning Breakfast Time

Here's to the piping porridge,
Here's to the biscuits hot,
Here's to the java
Flowing like lava
Out of the coffee pot.
Here's to the eggs and bacon,
Here's to the waffles unique,
And here's and here's
Three rousing cheers
For the best meal of the week!

For it's Sunday morning breakfast time,
The time all men adore!
Why don't the poets go into rhyme
And rave about it more?
For only then can a man forget
The sweat and the worries of his bane-
Ful lot as he calmly enjoys his toast
And most of Arthur Brisbane.
Breakfast time on other days
Means bolting at fever heat,
But on Sunday morning, there's the time
When a man has time to eat—and eat,
When a man has time to...
...Breakfast is served!

Lyrics and music by Cole Porter

Happy Birthday from Your Loving Brother

My sister plays with Barbie dolls.
She likes to wear a skirt.
Her room's so neat and tidy that
I think she's scared of dirt.

I know I cannot change her.
But I love to see her squirm.
And so on her next birthday
I am giving her a worm.

Bruce Lansky

Good-bye, Six—Hello, Seven

I'm getting a higher bunk bed.
And I'm getting a bigger bike.
And I'm getting to cross Connecticut Avenue
    all by myself, if I like.
And I'm getting to help do dishes.
And I'm getting to weed the yard.
And I'm getting to think that seven
    could be hard.

Judith Viorst

Half Birthday

Today's my half birthday!
I ran right into my parent's bed.
Dad grumbled, "It's half-past six."
Mom half-heartedly kissed me on the head.

I told my sister the big news.
Maybe today she won't be a pain.
But all she said was "How perfect—
Because you only have half a brain."

At school I wanted a crown.
This made my teacher laugh.
She gave me a crown all right—
Alas, she gave me half.

Mom says I should keep in mind
That the other half's coming up soon.
Then she pointed out my window...
There in the sky, a half moon!

Amy Krouse Rosenthal

If We Didn't Have Birthdays

If we didn't have birthdays, you wouldn't be you.
If you'd never been born, well then what would you do?
If you'd never been born, well then what would you be?
You *might* be a fish! Or a toad in a tree!
You might be a doorknob! Or three baked potatoes!
You might be a bag full of hard green tomatoes.
Or worse than all that...Why, you might be a WASN'T!
A Wasn't has no fun at all. No, he doesn't.
A Wasn't just isn't. He just isn't present.
But you...You ARE YOU! And, now isn't that pleasant!

Dr. Seuss

Brother

I had a little brother
And I brought him to my mother
And I said I want another
Little brother for a change.
But she said don't be a bother
So I took him to my father
And I said this little bother
Of a brother's very strange.
But he said one little brother
Is exactly like another
And every little brother
Misbehaves a bit he said.
So I took the little bother
From my mother and my father
And I put the little bother
Of a brother back to bed.

Mary Ann Hoberman

Six Weeks Old

He is so small, he does not know
The summer sun, the winter snow;
The spring that ebbs and comes again,
All this is far beyond his ken.

A little world he feels and sees:
His mother's arms, his mother's knees;
He hides his face against her breast,
And does not care to learn the rest.

Christopher Morley

Perambulator Poem

When I was christened
they held me up
and poured some water
out of a cup.

The trouble was
it fell on me,
and I and water
don't agree.

A lot of christeners
stood and listened:
I let them know
that I was christened.

David McCord

A Quiet Thing

When it all comes true,
Just the way you planned,
It's funny, but the bells don't ring.
It's a quiet thing.
When you hold the world
In your trembling hand,
You'd think you'd hear a choir sing.
It's a quiet thing.
There are no exploding fireworks
Where's the roaring of the crowds?
Maybe it's the strange new atmosphere,
'Way up here among the clouds.
But I don't hear the drums,
I don't hear the band,
The sounds I'm told such moments bring,
Happiness comes in on tiptoe.
Well, whatd'ya know!
It's a quiet thing,
A very quiet thing.

Lyrics and music by Fred Ebb and John Kander

Sunrise, Sunset

Is this the little girl I carried?
Is this the little boy at play?
I don't remember growing older.
When did they?
When did she get to be a beauty?
When did he grow to be so tall?
Wasn't it yesterday when they were small?

Sunrise, sunset,
Sunrise, sunset,
Swiftly flow the days;
Seedlings turn overnight to sunflow'rs,
Blossoming even as we gaze.

Sunrise, sunset,
Sunrise, sunset,
Swiftly fly the years;
One season following another,
Laden with happiness and tears.

Lyrics and music by Sheldon Harnick
and Jerry Bock
(Abridged version)

Nothing Like the Sun

A model of your standard you were not—
and though you had your charms, I must confess,
your breath was foul, your teeth were black with rot,
your oily skin discouraged a caress.

You lounged around, then slept all afternoon.
You wouldn't catch a ball and didn't swim.
The gas you passed could empty a saloon.
Your eyesight and intelligence were dim.

Perhaps your hair, a dirty shade of red,
accounted for some quirkiness and pluck.
You shredded Kleenex, stole and ate our bread,
and despite your Irish genes, had rotten luck.

This final epitaph might then surprise:
You were the apple of your mistress's eyes.

Emma Walton Hamilton

Death Is Nothing at All

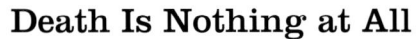

Death is nothing at all.
I have only slipped away to the next room.
I am I and you are you.
Whatever we were to each other,
That, we still are.

Call me by my old familiar name.
Speak to me in the easy way
which you always used.
Put no difference into your tone.
Wear no forced air of solemnity or sorrow.

Laugh as we always laughed
at the little jokes we enjoyed together.
Play, smile, think of me. Pray for me.
Let my name be ever the household word
that it always was.
Let it be spoken without effect.
Without the trace of a shadow on it.

Life means all that it ever meant.
It is the same that it ever was.
There is absolute unbroken continuity.
Why should I be out of mind
because I am out of sight?

I am but waiting for you.
For an interval.
Somewhere. Very near.
Just around the corner.

All is well.

Henry Scott Holland

If

If you can keep your head when all about you
　　Are losing theirs and blaming it on you;
If you can trust yourself when all men doubt you,
　　But make allowance for their doubting too:
If you can wait and not be tired by waiting,
　　Or, being lied about, don't deal in lies,
Or being hated don't give way to hating,
　　And yet don't look too good, nor talk too wise;

If you can dream—and not make dreams your master;
　　If you can think—and not make thoughts your aim,
If you can meet with Triumph and Disaster
　　And treat those two impostors just the same:
If you can bear to hear the truth you've spoken
　　Twisted by knaves to make a trap for fools,
Or watch the things you gave your life to, broken,
　　And stoop and build 'em up with worn-out tools;

If you can make one heap of all your winnings
　　And risk it on one turn of pitch-and-toss,
And lose, and start again at your beginnings,
　　And never breathe a word about your loss:
If you can force your heart and nerve and sinew
　　To serve your turn long after they are gone,
And so hold on when there is nothing in you
　　Except the Will which says to them: "Hold on!"

If you can talk with crowds and keep your virtue,
　　Or walk with Kings—nor lose the common touch,
If neither foes nor loving friends can hurt you,
　　If all men count with you, but none too much:
If you can fill the unforgiving minute
　　With sixty seconds' worth of distance run,
Yours is the Earth and everything that's in it,
　　And—which is more—you'll be a Man, my son!

Rudyard Kipling

May the road rise to meet you
Traditional Irish Folk Blessing

May the road rise up to meet you,
May the wind be always at your back,
May the sun shine warm on your face,
The rain fall softly on your fields,
And until we meet again
May God hold you in the palm of his hand.

Anonymous

Folami Abiade: "in daddy's arms" from *In Daddy's Arms I Am Tall: African Americans Celebrating Fathers*, reprinted with the permission of Lee & Low Books.

Carol Adler: "Havdalah" from *Poems for Jewish Holidays*, selected by Myra Cohn Livingston (New York: Holiday House, 1986), reprinted by permission of the author.

Herbert Asquith: "Skating," reprinted with the permission of Roland Asquith.

Sami Bentil: "Sacred Duty" from *The Complete Kwanzaa: Celebrating Our Cultural Harvest*, edited by Dorothy Winbush Riley (Castle Books, 2003), reprinted with the permission of the author.

Marchette Chute: "Our Tree," reprinted with the permission of the Estate of Marchette Chute.

Sandra Cisneros: "Good Hot Dogs" from *My Wicked Wicked Ways*, copyright © 1987 by Sandra Cisneros, published by Third Woman Press and in hardcover by Alfred A. Knopf, reprinted by permission of Third Woman Press and Susan Bergholz Literary Services, New York, all rights reserved.

Billy Collins: "Today" from *Poetry* (April 2000), copyright © 2000 by Billy Collins, reprinted by permission of SLL/Sterling Lord Literistic, Inc. for the author.

e. e. cummings: "little tree" from *E. E. Cummings: Complete Poems 1904–1962*, edited by George J. Firmage, copyright 1925, 1953, © 1991 by the Trustees for the E. E. Cummings Trust, copyright © 1976 by George James Firmage, used by permission of Liveright Publishing Corporation.

Helen Bayley Davis: "Jack Frost" from *The Christian Science Monitor* (January 14, 1929), courtesy of *The Christian Science Monitor* (www.csmonitor.com).

Walter de la Mare: "The Snowflake" from *The Complete Poems of Walter de la Mare* (New York: Knopf, 1970), reprinted with the permission of the Literary Trustees of Walter de la Mare and The Society of Authors as their representative.

Emily Dickinson: "The morns are meeker than they were (Autumn)" and "Bee, I'm expecting you!" from *The Poems of Emily Dickinson*, edited by Thomas H. Johnson, copyright 1945, 1951, © 1955, 1979, 1983 by the President and Fellows of Harvard College, reprinted with the permission of the Belknap Press of Harvard University Press.

Ivy O. Eastwick: "Thanksgiving" from *Cherry Stones! Garden Swings! Poems*, copyright © 1962 by Ivy O. Eastwick, renewed 1990 by Abingdon Press, used by permission.

Fred Ebb and John Kander: "A Quiet Thing," used by permission of Alley Music Corporation.

Barbara Juster Esbensen: "Cardinal," "First Day of School," "Nocturne for Late Summer," and "Now that Spring Is Here…" from *Cold Stars and Fireflies: Poems of the Four Seasons*, copyright © 1991 by Barbara Juster Esbensen; "The Fourteenth Day of Adar" from *Poems for Jewish Holidays*, selected by Myra Cohn Livingston (New York: Holiday House, 1986), copyright © 1986 by Barbara Juster Esbensen, reprinted with the permission of the Estate of Barbara Juster Esbensen; "Umbrellas" from *Swing Around the Sun*, text copyright © 1965 by Lerner Publications Company, © 2003 by Carolrhoda Books, Inc., reprinted with the permission of Carolrhoda Books, a division of Lerner Publishing Group, Inc., all rights reserved. No part of this excerpt may be used or reproduced in any manner whatsoever without the prior written permission of Lerner Publishing Group, Inc.

Eleanor Farjeon: "Morning has broken" from *Songs of Praise, Second Enlarged Edition* (Oxford University Press, 1931), reprinted with the permission of David Higham Associates, Ltd.

Acknowledgments

Karla Kuskin: "Spring" and "To You" from *Moon, Have You Met My Mother?: The Collected Poems of Karla Kuskin* (New York: HarperCollins, 2003), copyright © 1987 by Karla Kuskin, used by permission of Scott Treimel, NY.

Bruce Lansky: "Happy Birthday from Your Loving Brother" and "New Year's Resolutions" from *Poetry Party: Funny Poems*, copyright © 1996 by Bruce Lansky, reprinted with the permission of Meadowbrook Press.

J. Patrick Lewis: "Sand House" from *Earth Verses and Water Rhymes* (New York: Atheneum, 1991), copyright © 1991 by J. Patrick Lewis, reprinted by permission of Curtis Brown, Ltd.

Myra Cohn Livingston: "April Fool," "Martin Luther King Day," "New Year's Eve," and "Passover," from *Celebrations*, copyright © 1985 by Myra Cohn Livingston; "Kittens" from *Worlds I Know and Other Poems*, copyright © 1985 by Myra Cohn Livingston; "Reading: Summer" from *Remembering and Other Poems*, copyright © 1980, 1989 by Myra Cohn Livingston, reprinted by permission of Marian Reiner.

Alice Low: "Some Things About Grandpas" from *The Family Read-Aloud Holiday Treasury*, selected by Alice Low, copyright © by Alice Low, used by permission of Scott Treimel, NY.

Kam Mak: "New Year's Day!" from *My Chinatown: One Year in Poems*, copyright © 2002 by Kam Mak, used by permission of HarperCollins Publishers.

Richard J. Margolis: "How to Get Through the Memorial Service" from *Poems for the Jewish Holidays*, edited by Myra Cohn Livingston (Holiday House, 1986), reprinted with the permission of the Estate of Richard J. Margolis.

Mildred Meigs: "Abraham Lincoln" from *Child Life* (1936), copyright © 1936 by Children's Better Health Institute, The Saturday Evening Post Society, Inc., Indianapolis, Indiana, used by permission.

Johnny Mercer: "A Little Boy's Rainy Day" (1973), used by permission of The Johnny Mercer Foundation © 2009 The Johnny Mercer Foundation (Warner-Chappel, Administrator).

John Mole: "The Waiting Game" from *Catching the Spider* (Blackie Children's Books, 1990), copyright © by John Mole, reprinted with the permission of the author.

Helen H. Moore: "Chief Seattle's Lesson" from *A Poem a Day: 180 Thematic Poems and Activities that Teach and Delight All Year Long*, copyright © 1997 by Helen H. Moore, reprinted by permission of Scholastic, Inc.

Lilian Moore: "Ground Hog Day" from *Think of Shadows*, copyright © 1975, 1980 by Lilian Moore, reprinted by permission of Marian Reiner.

Pat Mora: "Dancing Paper" from *Confetti: Poems for Children*, copyright © 1999 by Pat Mora, reprinted with the permission of Lee & Low Books.

Ogden Nash: "Columbus," copyright 1938 by Ogden Nash, renewed, reprinted by permission of Curtis Brown, Ltd. and Carlton Publishing Group.

Robert Newton Peck: "Four of July" from *Bee Tree and Other Stuff* (New York: Walker, 1975), copyright © 1975 by Robert Newton Peck, reprinted with the permission of the author.

Harry Philip: "Rosh ha-Shanah Eve" from *Poems for the Jewish Holidays*, edited by Myra Cohn Livingston (Holiday House, 1986), reprinted with the permission of the Estate of Richard J. Margolis.